for People on the Go

compiled by
Randall and Susan Jahns

SHAW BOOKS
an imprint of WaterBrook Press

Promises for People on the Go
A Shaw Book
Published By WaterBrook Press
2375 Telstar Drive, Suite 160
Colorado Springs, CO 80920
A division of Random House, Inc.

ISBN: 0-87788-648-2

Compiled by Randall and Susan Jahns
Cover photo by Jim Wright

Printed in the United States of America
2001

05 04 03

Contents

Introduction

Today's world is full of challenges and exciting possibilities for you as you seek to follow Christ. Time, money, work, family, relationships, the future—all of these areas offer challenges and questions. But often in the busyness of life the challenges can seem too great and the questions impossible to answer.

God's Word is the perfect source of strength and daily food for you as you go about your everyday living. In the Bible you'll find guidelines for right living at home, at work, and in the world around you. God makes plain his desires for you as you relate to him and to others with whom you come in contact. And, as you discover his ways, you'll be challenged to avoid being squeezed into the mold of the world and to live a life that's pleasing to him.

Within this book are some principles from the Bible that relate to major areas of your life today. As you meditate on these passages, allow God to teach you, encourage you, correct you, and show you his loving plans for you.

"The whole Bible was given to us by inspiration from God and is useful to teach us what is true and to make us realize what is wrong in our lives; it straightens us out and helps us do what is right. It is God's way of making us well prepared at every point, fully equipped to do good to everyone." *2 Timothy 3:16-17,* TLB

Loving God

"The true measure of loving God is to love him without measure."

ST. BERNARD OF CLAIRVAUX

For God so loved the world that he gave his one and only Son, that whoever believes in him shall not perish but have eternal life. *John 3:16, NIV*

But because of his great love for us, God, who is rich in mercy, made us alive with Christ even when we were dead in transgressions—it is by grace you have been saved. *Ephesians 2:4-5, NIV*

For I am convinced that nothing can ever separate us from his love. Death can't, and life can't. The angels won't, and all the powers of hell itself cannot keep God's love away. Our fears for today, our worries about tomorrow, or where we are—high above the sky, or in the deepest ocean—nothing will ever be able to separate us from the love of God demonstrated by our Lord Jesus Christ when he died for us. *Romans 8:38-39, TLB*

But God demonstrates his own love for us in this: While we were still sinners, Christ died for us. *Romans 5:8,* NIV

"Just as the Father has loved Me, I have also loved you; abide in My love. *John 15:9,* NASB

The Lord appeared to us in the past, saying: "I have loved you with an everlasting love; I have drawn you with loving-kindness." *Jeremiah 31:3,* NIV

See how great a love the Father has bestowed upon us, that we should be called children of God; and such we are. For this reason the world does not know us, because it did not know Him. *1 John 3:1,* NASB

This is love: not that we loved God, but that he loved us and sent his Son as an atoning sacrifice for our sins. *1 John 4:10,* NIV

"Sir, which is the most important command in the laws of Moses?" Jesus replied, "'Love the Lord your God with all your heart and soul and mind.' This is the first and greatest commandment. The second most important is similar: 'Love your neighbor as much as you love yourself.' All the other commandments and all the demands of the prophets stem from these two laws and are fulfilled if you obey them. Keep only these and you will find that you are obeying all the others." *Matthew 22:36-40, TLB*

"If you love Me, you will keep My commandments." *John 14:15, NASB*

Jesus replied, "If anyone loves me, he will obey my teaching . . . These words you hear are not my own; they belong to the Father who sent me." *John 14:23-24, NIV*

And now, O Israel, what does the Lord your God ask of you but to fear the Lord your God, to walk in all his ways, to love him, to serve the Lord your God with all your heart and with all your soul, and to observe the Lord's commands and decrees that I am giving you today for your own good? *Deuteronomy 10:12-13, NIV*

He has told you, O man, what is good;
And what does the LORD
require of you
But to do justice, to love kindness,
And to walk humbly with your God?
Micah 6:8, NASB

Learning to Pray

"It is impossible for a believer, no matter what his experience, to keep right with God if he will not take the trouble to spend time with God."

OSWALD CHAMBERS

Be anxious for nothing, but in everything by prayer and supplication with thanksgiving let your requests be made known to God. And the peace of God, which surpasses all comprehension, shall guard your hearts and your minds in Christ Jesus. *Philippians 4:6-7,* NASB

So I want men everywhere to pray with holy hands lifted up to God, free from sin and anger and resentment. *1 Timothy 2:8,* TLB

Therefore I say to you, all things for which you pray and ask, believe that you have received them, and they shall be granted you. And whenever you stand praying, forgive, if you have anything against anyone; so that your Father who is in heaven may forgive you your transgressions. *Mark 11:24-25,* NASB

Therefore, confess your sins to each other and pray for each other so that you may be healed. The prayer of a righteous man is powerful and effective. *James 5:16,* NIV

"Keep watching and praying, that you may not enter into temptation; the spirit is willing, but the flesh is weak." *Matthew 26:41,* NASB

Until now you have not asked for anything in my name. Ask and you will receive, and your joy will be complete. *John 16:24,* NIV

"Then you will call upon me and come and pray to me, and I will listen to you. You will seek me and find me when you seek me with all your heart." *Jeremiah 29:12-13,* NIV

Devote yourselves to prayer, keeping alert in it with an attitude of thanksgiving . . . *Colossians 4:2,* NASB

And in the same way—by our faith—the Holy Spirit helps us with our daily problems and in our praying. For we don't even know what we should pray for, nor how to pray as we should; but the Holy Spirit prays for us with such feeling that it cannot be expressed in words. And the Father who knows all hearts knows, of course, what the Spirit is saying as he pleads for us in harmony with God's own will. *Romans 8:26-27,* TLB

I will pray morning, noon, and night, pleading aloud with God; and he will hear and answer. *Psalm 55:17,* TLB

Ask and it will be given to you; seek and you will find; knock and the door will be opened to you. For everyone who asks receives; he who seeks finds; and to him who knocks, the door will be opened. *Matthew 7:7-8,* NIV

Reading God's Word

"Apply yourself to the whole text, and apply the whole text to yourself."

JOHANNES ALBRECHT BENGEL

This book of the law shall not depart out of your mouth, but you shall meditate on it day and night, that you may be careful to do according to all that is written in it; for then you shall make your way prosperous, and then you shall have good success. *Joshua 1:8*, RSV

God's laws are perfect. They protect us, make us wise, and give us joy and light. God's laws are pure, eternal, just. They are more desirable than gold. They are sweeter than honey dripping from a honeycomb. For they warn us away from harm and give success to those who obey them. *Psalm 19:7-11*, TLB

Jesus answered, "It is written: 'Man does not live on bread alone, but on every word that comes from the mouth of God.' " *Matthew 4:4*, NIV

How blessed is the man who does not
walk in the counsel of the wicked,
Nor stand in the path of sinners,

Nor sit in the seat of scoffers!
But his delight is in the law of
the LORD,
And in His law he meditates day
and night.
And he will be like a tree firmly planted by streams of water,
Which yields its fruit in its season,
And its leaf does not wither;
And in whatever he does, he prospers.
Psalm 1:1-3, NASB

Anyone who listens to the word but does not do what it says is like a man who looks at his face in a mirror and, after looking at himself, goes away and immediately forgets what he looks like. But the man who looks intently into the perfect law that gives freedom, and continues to do this, not forgetting what he has heard, but doing it—he will be blessed in what he does. *James 1:23-25*, NIV

How can a young man stay pure? By reading your Word and following its rules. I have tried my best to find you—don't let me wander off from your instructions. I have thought much about your words, and stored them in my heart so that they would hold me back from sin. *Psalm 119:9-11*, TLB

Your words are what sustain me; they are food to my hungry soul. They bring joy to my sorrowing heart and delight me. How proud I am to bear your name, O Lord. *Jeremiah 15:16*, TLB

Your word is a lamp to my feet and a light for my path. *Psalm 119:105*, NIV

For the word of God is living and active and sharper than any two-edged sword, and piercing as far as the division of soul and spirit, of both joints and marrow, and able to judge the thoughts and intentions of the heart. *Hebrews 4:12*, NASB

Heaven and earth will pass away, but my words will never pass away. *Matthew 24:35*, NIV

As the rain and snow come down from heaven and stay upon the ground to water the earth, and cause the grain to grow and to produce seed for the farmer and bread for the hungry, so also is my Word. I send it out and it always produces fruit. It shall accomplish all I want it to, and prosper everywhere I send it. *Isaiah 55:10-11,* TLB

For whatever was written in earlier times was written for our instruction, that through perseverance and the encouragement of the Scriptures we might have hope. *Romans 15:4,* NASB

Taking Root

"I have a great need for Christ; I have a great Christ for my need."

CHARLES HADDON SPURGEON

And now just as you trusted Christ to save you, trust him, too, for each day's problems; live in vital union with him. Let your roots grow down into him and draw up nourishment from him. See that you go on growing in the Lord, and become strong and vigorous in the truth you were taught. Let your lives overflow with joy and thanksgiving for all he has done. *Colossians 2:6-7, TLB*

Know therefore that the LORD your God is God; he is the faithful God, keeping his covenant of love to a thousand generations of those who love him and keep his commands. *Deuteronomy 7:9, NIV*

How blessed is the man who does not
walk in the counsel of the wicked,
Nor stand in the path of sinners,
Nor sit in the seat of scoffers!
But his delight is in the law of
the LORD,
And in His law he meditates day
and night.

And he will be like a tree firmly
planted by streams of water,
Which yields its fruit in its season,
And its leaf does not wither;
And in whatever he does, he prospers.
Psalm 1:1-3, NASB

For this God is our God for ever and ever; he will be our guide even to the end. *Psalm 48:14,* NIV

Before the mountains were born or you brought forth the earth and the world, from everlasting to everlasting you are God. *Psalm 90:2,* NIV

But Thou art the same,
And Thy years will not come
to an end.
Psalm 102:27, NASB

Now may our Lord Jesus Christ Himself and God our Father, who has loved us and given us eternal comfort and good hope by grace, comfort and strengthen your hearts in every good work and word. *2 Thessalonians 2:16-17,* NASB

Jesus Christ is the same yesterday and today and forever. *Hebrews 13:8*, NIV

But whatever is good and perfect comes to us from God, the Creator of all light, and he shines forever without change or shadow. *James 1:17*, *TLB*

And He shall be the stability of
your times,
A wealth of salvation, wisdom,
and knowledge;
The fear of the LORD is his treasure.
Isaiah 33:6, NASB

Abiding in Christ

"There are many in the Church as well as out of it who need to learn that Christianity is neither a creed nor a ceremonial, but a life vitally connected with a loving Christ."

JOSIAH STRONG

"Abide in me, and I in you. As the branch cannot bear fruit of itself, unless it abides in the vine, so neither can you, unless you abide in Me. I am the vine, you are the branches; he who abides in Me, and I in him, he bears much fruit; for apart from Me you can do nothing." *John 15:4-5, NASB*

Therefore, I urge you, brothers, in view of God's mercy, to offer yourselves as living sacrifices, holy and pleasing to God—which is your spiritual worship. Do not conform any longer to the pattern of this world, but be transformed by the renewing of your mind. Then you will be able to test and approve what God's will is—his good, pleasing and perfect will. *Romans 12:1-2, NIV*

He replied, "Blessed rather are those who hear the word of God and obey it." *Luke 11:28, NIV*

"If you love Me, you will keep My commandments." *John 14:15, NASB*

For, dear brothers, you have been given freedom: not freedom to do wrong, but freedom to love and serve each other. *Galatians 5:13,* TLB

Lead me in Thy truth and teach me,
For Thou art the God of my salvation;
For Thee I wait all the day. *Psalm 25:5, NASB*

Therefore, prepare your minds for action; be self-controlled; set your hope fully on the grace to be given you when Jesus Christ is revealed. As obedient children, do not conform to the evil desires you had when you lived in ignorance. But just as he who called you is holy, so be holy in all you do; for it is written: "Be holy, because I am holy." *1 Peter 1:13-16,* NIV

Flee the evil desires of youth, and pursue righteousness, faith, love and peace, along with those who call on the Lord out of a pure heart. *2 Timothy 2:22,* NIV

Remember what Christ taught and let his words enrich your lives and make you wise; teach them to each other and sing them out in psalms and hymns and spiritual songs, singing to the Lord with thankful hearts. *Colossians 3:16,* TLB

For this is the love of God, that we keep His commandments; and His commandments are not burdensome. *1 John 5:3,* NASB

We know that we live in him and he in us, because he has given us of his Spirit. *1 John 4:13,* NIV

And now, dear children, continue in him, so that when he appears we may be confident and unashamed before him at his coming. *1 John 2:28,* NIV

Relating to Others

"If thou neglectest thy love to thy neighbor, in vain thou professest thy love to God; for by thy love to God, the love to thy neighbor is begotten, and by the love to thy neighbor, thy love to God is nourished."

FRANCIS QUARLES

Little children, let us stop just saying we love people; let us really love them, and show it by our actions. *1 John 3:18*, TLB

Dear brothers, don't ever forget that it is best to listen much, speak little, and not become angry; for anger doesn't make us good, as God demands that we must be. *James 1:19-20*, TLB

And the seed whose fruit is righteousness is sown in peace by those who make peace. *James 3:18*, NASB

Again I say, don't get involved in foolish arguments which only upset people and make them angry. God's people must not be quarrelsome; they must be gentle, patient teachers of those who are wrong. Be humble when you are trying to teach those who are mixed up concerning the truth. For if you talk meekly and courteously to them they are more likely, with God's help, to turn away from their wrong ideas and believe what is true. *2 Timothy 2:23-25*, TLB

No one has beheld God at any time; if we love one another, God abides in us, and His love is perfected in us. *1 John 4:12,* NASB

But concerning the pure brotherly love that there should be among God's people, I don't need to say very much, I'm sure! For God himself is teaching you to love one another. Indeed, your love is already strong toward all the Christian brothers throughout your whole nation. Even so, dear friends, we beg you to love them more and more. *1 Thessalonians 4:9-10,* TLB

In response to all he has done for us, let us outdo each other in being helpful and kind to each other and in doing good. *Hebrews 10:24,* TLB

Whoever loves his brother lives in the light, and there is nothing in him to make him stumble. *1 John 2:10,* NIV

Now you can have real love for everyone because your souls have been cleansed from selfishness and hatred when you trusted Christ to save you; so see to it that you really do love each other warmly, with all your hearts. *1 Peter 1:22*, TLB

Let love be without hypocrisy. Abhor what is evil; cleave to what is good. Be devoted to one another in brotherly love; give preference to one another in honor . . . *Romans 12:9-10*, NASB

Finally, all of you, live in harmony with one another; be sympathetic, love as brothers, be compassionate and humble. *1 Peter 3:8, NIV*

Hatred stirs old quarrels, but love overlooks insults. *Proverbs 10:12, TLB*

Don't seek vengeance. Don't bear a grudge; but love your neighbor as yourself, for I am Jehovah. *Leviticus 19:18, TLB*

Be kind and compassionate to one another, forgiving each other, just as in Christ God forgave you. *Ephesians 4:32, NIV*

Therefore, as God's chosen people, holy and dearly loved, clothe yourselves with compassion, kindness, humility, gentleness and patience. Bear with each other and forgive whatever grievances you may have against one another. Forgive as the Lord forgave you. And over all these virtues put on love, which binds them all together in perfect unity. *Colossians 3:12-14, NIV*

Sharing the Good News

"The church has many tasks but only one mission."

ARTHUR PRESTON

Then Jesus came to them and said, "All authority in heaven and on earth has been given to me. Therefore go and make disciples of all nations, baptizing them in the name of the Father and of the Son and of the Holy Spirit, and teaching them to obey everything I have commanded you. And surely I will be with you always, to the very end of the age." *Matthew 28:18-20,* NIV

But in your hearts acknowledge Christ as the holy Lord. Always be prepared to give an answer to everyone who asks you to give the reason for the hope that you have. But do this with gentleness and respect, keeping a clear conscience, so that those who speak maliciously against your good behavior in Christ may be ashamed of their slander. *1 Peter 3:15-16,* NIV

Make the most of your chances to tell others the Good News. Be wise in all your contacts with them. Let your conversation be gracious as well as sensible, for then you will have the right answer for everyone. *Colossians 4:5-6,* TLB

Make it your ambition to lead a quiet life, to mind your own business and to work with your hands, just as we told you, so that your daily life may win the respect of outsiders and so that you will not be dependent on anybody. *1 Thessalonians 4:11-12,* NIV

. . . for "WHOEVER WILL CALL UPON THE NAME OF THE LORD WILL BE SAVED." How then shall they call upon Him in whom they have not believed? And how shall they believe in Him whom they have not heard? And how shall they hear without a preacher? *Romans 10:13-14,* NASB

Be careful how you behave among your unsaved neighbors; for then, even if they are suspicious of you and talk against you, they will end up praising God for your good works when Christ returns. *1 Peter 2:12,* TLB

For God did not give us a spirit of timidity, but a spirit of power, of love and of self-discipline. So do not be ashamed to testify about our Lord . . . *2 Timothy 1:7-8,* NIV

However, I consider my life worth nothing to me, if only I may finish the race and complete the task the Lord Jesus has given me—the task of testifying to the gospel of God's grace. *Acts 20:24,* NIV

For I am not ashamed of the gospel, for it is the power of God for salvation to every one who believes, to the Jew first and also to the Greek. *Romans 1:16,* NASB

We proclaim to you what we have seen and heard, so that you also may have fellowship with us. And our fellowship is with the Father and with his Son, Jesus Christ. *1 John 1:3,* NIV

How beautiful upon the mountains are the feet of those who bring the

happy news of peace and salvation, the news that the God of Israel reigns.
Isaiah 52:7, TLB

Caring for the World

"Biblical orthodoxy without compassion is surely the ugliest thing in the world."

FRANCIS SCHAEFFER

If there is a poor man among your brothers in any of the towns of the land that the Lord your God is giving you, do not be hardhearted or tightfisted toward your poor brother. Rather be openhanded and freely lend him whatever he needs. *Deuteronomy 15:7-8,* NIV

How blessed is he who considers
  the helpless;
The LORD will deliver him in a day
  of trouble. *Psalm 41:1,* NASB

Give to one who asks you, and do not turn away from the one who wants to borrow from you. *Matthew 5:42,* NIV

But whoever has the world's goods, and beholds his brother in need and closes his heart against him, how does the love of God abide in Him? Little children, let us not love with word or with tongue, but in deed and truth. We shall know by this that we are of the truth, and shall assure our heart before Him. *1 John 3:17-19,* NASB

When you help the poor you are lending to the Lord—and he pays wonderful interest on your loan! *Proverbs 19:17*, TLB

Now that you have purified yourselves by obeying the truth so that you have sincere love for your brothers, love one another deeply, with all your hearts. *1 Peter 1:22*, NIV

For God is not unjust so as to forget your work and the love which you have shown toward His name, in having ministered and in still ministering to the saints. *Hebrews 6:10*, *NASB*

. . . and if you spend yourselves in behalf of the hungry and satisfy the needs of the oppressed, then your light will rise in the darkness, and your night will become like the noonday. The LORD will guide you always; he will satisfy your needs in a sun-scorched land and will strengthen your frame. You will be like a well-watered garden, like a spring whose waters never fail. *Isaiah 58:10-11,* NIV

This is what the LORD says: "Let not the wise man boast of his wisdom or the strong man boast of his strength or the rich man boast of his riches, but let him who boasts boast about this: that he understands and knows me, that I am the LORD, who exercises kindness, justice and righteousness on earth, for in these I delight," declares the LORD. *Jeremiah 9:23-24,* NIV

You are the light of the world. A city set on a hill cannot be hidden . . . Let your light shine before men in such a way that they may see your good works, and glorify your Father who is in heaven. *Matthew 5:14,16,* NASB

In everything, do to others what you would have them do to you, for this sums up the Law and the Prophets. *Matthew 7:12,* NIV

Guarding Your Mind

"If you would voyage Godward, you must see to it that the rudder of thought is right."

W. J. DAWSON

Finally, brethren, whatever is true, whatever is honorable, whatever is right, whatever is pure, whatever is lovely, whatever is of good repute, if there is any excellence and if anything worthy of praise, let your mind dwell on these things. *Philippians 4:8,* NASB

Set your minds on things above, not on earthly things. For you died, and your life is now hidden with Christ in God. *Colossians 3:2-3,* NIV

Those who live according to the sinful nature have their minds set on what that nature desires; but those who live in accordance with the Spirit have their minds set on what the Spirit desires. The mind of sinful man is death, but the mind controlled by the Spirit is life and peace... *Romans 8:5-6,* *NIV*

For whatever God says to us is full of living power: it is sharper than the sharpest dagger, cutting swift and deep into our innermost thoughts and desires with all their parts, exposing us for what we really are. *Hebrews 4:12,* TLB

Do not conform any longer to the pattern of this world, but be transformed by the renewing of your mind. Then you will be able to test and approve what God's will is—his good, pleasing and perfect will. *Romans 12:2,* NIV

This plan of mine is not what you would work out, neither are my thoughts the same as yours! For just as the heavens are higher than the earth, so are my ways higher than yours, and my thoughts than yours. *Isaiah 55:8-9,* TLB

The LORD knows the thoughts of man,
That they are a mere breath.
Psalm 94:11, NASB

As for you, my son Solomon, know the God of your father, and serve Him with a whole heart and willing mind; for the LORD searches all hearts, and understands every intent of the thoughts. If you seek Him, He will let you find Him; but if you forsake Him, He will reject you forever. *1 Chronicles 28:9, NASB*

Run from anything that gives you the evil thoughts that young men often have, but stay close to anything that makes you want to do right. Have faith and love, and enjoy the companionship of those who love the Lord and have pure hearts. *2 Timothy 2:22, TLB*

Therefore, prepare your minds for action; be self-controlled; set your hope fully on the grace to be given you when Jesus Christ is revealed. *1 Peter 1:13, NIV*

I have hidden your word in my heart that I might not sin against you. *Psalm 119:11, NIV*

Resisting Temptation

"Temptations that find us dwelling in God are to our faith like winds that more firmly root the tree."

ANONYMOUS

No temptation has seized you except what is common to man. And God is faithful; he will not let you be tempted beyond what you can bear. But when you are tempted, he will also provide a way out so that you can stand up under it. *1 Corinthians 10:13,* NIV

Let no one say when he is tempted, "I am being tempted by God"; for God cannot be tempted by evil, and He Himself does not tempt any one. But each one is tempted when he is carried away and enticed by his own lust. Then when lust has conceived, it gives birth to sin; and when sin is accomplished, it brings forth death. *James 1:13-15,* NASB

How can a young man stay pure? By reading your Word and following its rules. I have tried my best to find you—don't let me wander off from your instructions. I have thought much about your words, and stored them in my heart so that they would hold me back from sin. *Psalm 119:9-11,* TLB

But you, man of God, flee from all this, and pursue righteousness, godliness, faith, love, endurance and gentleness. *1 Timothy 6:11,* NIV

But the Lord is faithful, and he will strengthen and protect you from the evil one. *2 Thessalonians 3:3,* NIV

Blessed is a man who perseveres under trial; for once he has been approved, he will receive the crown of life, which the Lord has promised to those who love Him. *James 1:12,* NASB

And do not lead us into temptation, but deliver us from evil . . . *Matthew 6:13a,* NASB

Since then we have a great high priest who has passed through the heavens, Jesus the Son of God, let us hold fast our confession. For we do not have a high priest who cannot sympathize with our weaknesses, but one who has been tempted in all things as we are, yet without sin. Let us therefore draw near with confidence to the throne of grace, that we may receive mercy and may find grace to help in time of need. *Hebrews 4:14-16,* NASB

Submit yourselves, then, to God. Resist the devil, and he will flee from you. Come near to God and he will come near to you. Wash your hands, you sinners, and purify your hearts, you double-minded. *James 4:7-8,* NIV

Keep alert and pray. Otherwise temptation will overpower you. For the spirit indeed is willing, but how weak the body is! *Matthew 26:41* TLB

Run from anything that gives you the evil thoughts that young men often have, but stay close to anything that makes you want to do right. Have faith and love, and enjoy the companionship of those who love the Lord and have pure hearts. 2 *Timothy 2:22,* TLB

Therefore, prepare your minds for action; be self-controlled; set your hope fully on the grace to be given you when Jesus Christ is revealed. As obedient children, do not conform to the evil desires you had when you lived in ignorance. But just as he who called you is holy, so be holy in all you do; for it is written: "Be holy, because I am holy." *1 Peter 1:13-16, NIV*

Enjoying Work

"I ask that work should be looked upon, not as a necessary drudgery to be undergone for the purpose of making money, but as a way of life in which the nature of man should find its proper exercise and delight and so fulfill itself to the glory of God."

DOROTHY L. SAYERS

Whatever you do, do your work heartily, as for the Lord rather than for men; knowing that from the Lord you will receive the reward of the inheritance. It is the Lord Christ whom you serve. *Colossians 3:23-24*, NASB

Do you see a man skilled in his work? He will serve before kings; he will not serve before obscure men. *Proverbs 22:29*, NIV

Never be lazy in your work but serve the Lord enthusiastically. *Romans 12:11*, TLB

Do your best to present yourself to God as one approved, a workman who does not need to be ashamed and who correctly handles the word of truth. *2 Timothy 2:15*, NIV

Whatever your hands find to do, do it with all your might, for in the grave, where you are going, there is neither working nor planning nor knowledge nor wisdom. *Ecclesiastes 9:10*, NIV

God is not unjust; he will not forget your work and the love you have shown him as you have helped his people and continue to help them. We want each of you to show this same diligence to the very end, in order to make your hope sure. We do not want you to become lazy, but to imitate those who through faith and patience inherit what has been promised. *Hebrews 6:10-12,* NIV

Obey your leaders and submit to their authority. They keep watch over you as men who must give an account. Obey them so that their work will be a joy, not a burden, for that would be of no advantage to you. *Hebrews 13:17,* NIV

The sluggard craves and gets nothing, but the desires of the diligent are fully satisfied. *Proverbs 13:4,* NIV

The man who works hard sleeps well whether he eats little or much, but the rich must worry and suffer insomnia. *Ecclesiastes 5:12,* TLB

He who is faithful in a very little thing is faithful also in much; and he who is unrighteous in a very little thing is unrighteous also in much. *Luke 16:10, NASB*

Commit to the Lord whatever you do, and your plans will succeed. *Proverbs 16:3,* NIV

And the Lord replied, "I myself will go with you and give you success." *Exodus 33:14,* TLB

Commit everything you do to the Lord. Trust him to help you do it and he will. *Psalm 37:5,* TLB

Serving Others

"A Christian man is the most free lord of all, and subject to none; a Christian man is the most dutiful servant of all, and subject to everyone."

MARTIN LUTHER

Love each other with brotherly affection and take delight in honoring each other. *Romans 12:10, TLB*

Each one should use whatever gift he has received to serve others, faithfully administering God's grace in its various forms. If anyone speaks, he should do it as one speaking the very words of God. If anyone serves, he should do it with the strength God provides, so that in all things God may be praised through Jesus Christ. To him be the glory and the power for ever and ever. Amen. *1 Peter 4:10-11, NIV*

Now the most important thing about a servant is that he does just what his master tells him to. *1 Corinthians 4:2, TLB*

"But if serving the Lord seems undesirable to you, then choose for yourselves this day whom you will serve, whether the gods your forefathers served beyond the River, or the gods of the Amorites, in whose land you are living. But as for me and my household, we will serve the LORD." *Joshua 24:15,* NIV

For, dear brothers, you have been given freedom: not freedom to do wrong, but freedom to love and serve each other. *Galatians 5:13, TLB*

Do nothing out of selfish ambition or vain conceit, but in humility consider others better than yourselves. Each of you should look not only to your own interests, but also to the interests of others. Your attitude should be the same as that of Christ Jesus: Who, being in very nature God, did not consider equality with God something to be grasped, but made himself nothing, taking the very nature of a servant, being made in human likeness. And being found in appearance as a man, he humbled himself and became obedient to death—even death on a cross! *Philippians 2:3-8, NIV*

Work hard, so God can say to you, "Well done." Be a good workman, one who does not need to be ashamed when God examines your work. Know what his Word says and means. *2 Timothy 2:15, TLB*

Each time he said, "No. But I am with you; that is all you need. My power shows up best in weak people." Now I am glad to boast about how weak I am; I am glad to be a living demonstration of Christ's power, instead of showing off my own power and abilities. *2 Corinthians 12:9, TLB*

This is My commandment, that you love one another, just as I have loved you. Greater love has no one than this, that one lay down his life for his friends. *John 15:12-13, NASB*

Living with Integrity

"People may doubt what you say, but they will always believe what you do."
ANONYMOUS

Do not lie to each other, since you have taken off your old self with its practices and have put on the new self, which is being renewed in knowledge in the image of its Creator. *Colossians 3:9-10,* NIV

Instead, speaking the truth in love, we will in all things grow up into him who is the Head, that is, Christ. *Ephesians 4:15,* NIV

Behold, Thou dost desire truth in the
innermost being,
And in the hidden part Thou wilt
make me know wisdom.
Psalm 51:6, NASB

For such is the will of God that by doing right you may silence the ignorance of foolish men. *1 Peter 2:15,* NASB

A good man hates lies; wicked men lie constantly and come to shame. A man's goodness helps him all through life, while evil men are being destroyed by their wickedness. *Proverbs 13:5-6*, TLB

The night is far gone, the day of his return will soon be here. So quit the evil deeds of darkness and put on the armor of right living, as we who live in the daylight should! Be decent and true in everything you do so that all can approve your behavior. *Romans 13:12-13a*, TLB

For unless you are honest in small matters, you won't be in large ones. If you cheat even a little, you won't be honest with greater responsibilities. *Luke 16:10*, TLB

The man of integrity walks securely, but he who takes crooked paths will be found out. *Proverbs 10:9*, NIV

Don't copy the behavior and customs of this world, but be a new and different person with a fresh newness in all you do and think. Then you will learn from your own experience how his ways will really satisfy you. *Romans 12:2, TLB*

The LORD abhors dishonest scales, but accurate weights are his delight . . . The integrity of the upright guides them, but the unfaithful are destroyed by their duplicity. *Proverbs 11:1, 3, NIV*

Righteousness guards the one whose
    way is blameless,
But wickedness subverts the sinner.
Proverbs 13:6, NASB

Let love and faithfulness never leave you; bind them around your neck, write them on the tablet of your heart. Then you will win favor and a good name in the sight of God and man. *Proverbs 3:3-4, NIV*

Handling Possessions

"The real measure of our wealth is how much we'd be worth if we lost all our money."

JOHN HENRY JOWETT

Let your way of life be free from the love of money, being content with what you have; for He Himself has said "I WILL NEVER DESERT YOU, NOR WILL I EVER FORSAKE YOU." *Hebrews 13:5, NASB*

The brother in humble circumstances ought to take pride in his high position. But the one who is rich should take pride in his low position, because he will pass away like a wild flower. For the sun rises with scorching heat and withers the plant; its blossom falls and its beauty is destroyed. In the same way, the rich man will fade away even while he goes about his business. *James 1:9-11, NIV*

Better a little with the fear of the LORD than great wealth with turmoil. *Proverbs 15:16, NIV*

But godliness with contentment is great gain. For we brought nothing into the world, and we can take nothing out of it. But if we have food and clothing, we will be content with that. People who want to get rich fall into temptation and a trap and into many foolish and harmful desires that plunge men into ruin and destruction. For the love of money is a root of all kinds of evil. Some people, eager for money, have wandered from the faith and pierced themselves with many griefs. *1 Timothy 6:6-10,* NIV

Don't weary yourself trying to get rich. Why waste your time? For riches can disappear as though they had the wings of a bird! *Proverbs 23:4-5,* TLB

Your riches won't help you on Judgment Day; only righteousness counts then. *Proverbs 11:4,* TLB

Trust in your money and down you go! Trust in God and flourish as a tree! *Proverbs 11:28,* TLB

The blessing of the LORD brings wealth, and he adds no trouble to it. *Proverbs 10:22,* NIV

Honor the LORD from your wealth,
And from the first of all your produce;
So your barns will be filled
with plenty,
And your vats will overflow with
new wine.
Proverbs 3:9-10, NASB

"I tell you the truth," Jesus replied, "no one who has left home or brothers or sisters or mother or father or children or fields for me and the gospel will fail to receive a hundred times as much in this present age (homes, brothers, sisters, mothers, children and fields—and with them, persecutions) and in the age to come, eternal life. *Mark 10:29-30, NIV*

"For this reason I say to you, do not be anxious for your life, as to what you shall eat, or what you shall drink; nor for your body, as to what you shall put on. Is not life more than food, and the body than clothing? . . . But seek first His kingdom and His righteousness; and all these things shall be added to you. Therefore do not be anxious for tomorrow; for tomorrow will care for itself. Each day has enough trouble of its own. *Matthew 6:25, 33-34,* NASB

Tell those who are rich not to be proud and not to trust in their money, which will soon be gone, but their pride and trust should be in the living God who always richly gives us all we need for our enjoyment. Tell them to use their money to do good. They should be rich in good works and should give happily to those in need, always being ready to share with others whatever God has given them. By doing this they will be storing up real treasure for themselves in heaven—it is the only safe investment for eternity! And they will be living a fruitful Christian life down here as well. *1 Timothy 6:17-19,* TLB

"Do not lay up for yourselves treasures upon earth, where moth and rust destroy, and where thieves break in and steal; but lay up for yourselves treasures in heaven, where neither moth nor rust destroys, and where thieves do not break in or steal; for where you treasure is, there will your heart be also." *Matthew 6:19-21,* NASB

Gaining Strength

"Lord, either lighten my burden or strengthen my back."

THOMAS FULLER

God is our refuge and strength, an ever-present help in trouble. *Psalm 46:1,* NIV

He gives strength to the weary and increases the power of the weak. Even youths grow tired and weary and young men stumble and fall; but those who hope in the LORD will renew their strength. They will soar on wings like eagles; they will run and not grow weary, they will walk and not be faint. *Isaiah 40:29-31,* NIV

The Sovereign Lord is my strength; he makes my feet like the feet of a deer, he enables me to go on the heights. *Habakkuk 3:19,* NIV

Trust in the Lord God always, for in the Lord Jehovah is your everlasting strength. *Isaiah 26:4,* TLB

And He has said to me, "My grace is sufficient for you, for power is perfected in weakness." Most gladly, therefore, I will rather boast about my weaknesses, that the power of Christ may dwell in me. *2 Corinthians 12:9,* NASB

Last of all I want to remind you that your strength must come from the Lord's mighty power within you. *Ephesians 6:10,* TLB

I can do everything through him who gives me strength. *Philippians 4:13,* NIV

For indeed He was crucified because of weakness, yet He lives because of the power of God. For we also are weak in Him, yet we shall live with Him because of the power of God directed toward you. *2 Corinthians 13:4,* NASB

You are awesome, O God, in your sanctuary; the God of Israel gives power and strength to his people. Praise be to God! *Psalm 68:35,* NIV

Fear not, for I am with you. Do not be dismayed. I am your God. I will strengthen you; I will help you; I will uphold you with my victorious right hand. *Isaiah 41:10,* TLB

Come to Me, all who are weary and heavy laden, and I will give you rest. *Matthew 11:28,* NASB

Blessed are those whose strength is in you, who have set their hearts on pilgrimage. *Psalm 84:5,* NIV

Finding Peace

"Worry does not empty tomorrow of its sorrow; it empties today of its strength."

CORRIE TEN BOOM

Let him have all your worries and cares, for he is always thinking about you and watching everything that concerns you. *1 Peter 5:7,* TLB

Yet the LORD longs to be gracious to you; he rises to show you compassion. For the LORD is a God of justice. Blessed are all who wait for him! *Isaiah 30:18,* NIV

You will keep in perfect peace him whose mind is steadfast, because he trusts in you. Trust in the LORD forever, for the LORD, the LORD, is the Rock eternal. *Isaiah 26:3-4,* NIV

I lie down and sleep; I wake again, because the LORD sustains me. *Psalm 3:5,* NIV

And we know that God causes all things to work together for good to those who love God, to those who are called according to His purpose. *Romans 8:28,* NASB

But now, thus says the LORD, your
Creator, O Jacob,
And He who formed you, O Israel:
"Do not fear, for I have redeemed you;
I have called you by name;
you are Mine!
When you pass through the waters,
I will be with you;
And through the rivers, they will not
overflow you.
When you walk through the fire,
you will not be scorched . . .

Isaiah 43:1-2, NASB

For the mind set on the flesh is death, but the mind set on the Spirit is life and peace . . . *Romans 8:6, NASB*

Then Jesus said to his disciples: "Therefore I tell you, do not worry about your life, what you will eat; or about your body, what you will wear. Life is more than food, and the body more than clothes . . . Who of you by worrying can add a single hour to his life? *Luke 12:22-23, 25, NIV*

You are my hiding place from every storm of life; you even keep me from getting into trouble! You surround me with songs of victory. *Psalm 32:7,* TLB

O Lord my God, many and many a time you have done great miracles for us, and we are ever in your thoughts. Who else can do such glorious things? No one else can be compared with you. There isn't time to tell of all your wonderful deeds. *Psalm 40:5,* TLB

The LORD himself goes before you and will be with you; he will never leave you nor forsake you. Do not be afraid; do not be discouraged. *Deuteronomy 31:8,* NIV

Peace I leave with you; My peace I give to you; not as the world gives, do I give to you. Let not your heart be troubled, nor let it be fearful. *John 14:27,* NASB

Resting in God

"Every morning I open the window for my King's grace, and every evening I sleep on the pillow of his love and care."
CELTIC SAINT

The LORD is my shepherd, I shall not be in want. He makes me lie down in green pastures, he leads me beside quiet waters, he restores my soul . . . *Psalm 23:1-3a,* NIV

Dear brothers, is your life full of difficulties and temptations? Then be happy, for when the way is rough, your patience has a chance to grow. So let it grow, and don't try to squirm out of your problems. For when your patience is finally in full bloom, then you will be ready for anything, strong in character, full and complete. *James 1:2-4,* TLB

Do not fear, for I am with you;
Do not anxiously look about you,
  for I am your God.
I will strengthen you,
  surely I will help you,
Surely I will uphold you with
  My righteous right hand.
Isaiah 41:10, NASB

So let us come boldly to the very throne of God and stay there to receive his mercy and to find grace to help us in our times of need. *Hebrews 4:16,* TLB

Cast all your anxiety on him because he cares for you. *1 Peter 5:7,* NIV

Be anxious for nothing, but in everything by prayer and supplication with thanksgiving let your requests be made known to God. And the peace of God, which surpasses all comprehension, shall guard your hearts and your minds in Christ Jesus. *Philippians 4:6-7,* NASB

I can do everything through him who gives me strength. *Philippians 4:13,* NIV

Come to Me, all who are weary and heavy laden, and I will give you rest. *Matthew 11:28,* NASB

I have told you all this so that you will have peace of heart and mind. Here on earth you will have many trials and sorrows; but cheer up, for I have overcome the world. *John 16:33,* TLB

Those who love Thy law
    have great peace,
And nothing causes them to stumble.
Psalm 119:165, NASB

Search me, O God, and know my heart: test me and know my anxious thoughts. See if there is any offensive way in me, and lead me in the way everlasting. *Psalm 139:23-24,* NIV

He will never let me stumble, slip or fall. For he is always watching, never sleeping. Jehovah himself is caring for you! He is your defender. He protects you day and night. He keeps you from all evil, and preserves your life. He keeps his eye upon you as you come and go, and always guards you. *Psalm 121:3-8,* TLB

I am with you and will watch over you wherever you go, and I will bring you back to this land. I will not leave you until I have done what I have promised you. *Genesis 28:15,* NIV

And He shall be the stability
of your times,
A wealth of salvation, wisdom,
and knowledge;
The fear of the LORD is his treasure.
Isaiah 33:6, NASB

I will lie down and sleep in peace, for you alone, O LORD, make me dwell in safety. *Psalm 4:8,* NIV

Overcoming Doubt

"Never doubt in the dark what God told you in the light."

V. RAYMOND EDMAN

Even when we are too weak to have any faith left, he remains faithful to us and will help us, for he cannot disown us who are part of himself, and he will always carry out his promises to us. *2 Timothy 2:13*, TLB

Because of his kindness you have been saved through trusting Christ. And even trusting is not of yourselves; it too is a gift from God. *Ephesians 2:8*, TLB

You will seek me and find me; when you seek me with all your heart, I will be found by you, says the Lord. *Jeremiah 29:13-14*, RSV

For I am convinced that neither death, nor life, nor angels, nor principalities, nor things present, nor things to come, nor powers, nor height, nor depth, nor any other created thing, shall be able to separate us from the love of God, which is in Christ Jesus our Lord. *Romans 8:38-39*, NASB

He is the Rock. His work is perfect. Everything he does is just and fair. He is faithful, without sin. *Deuteronomy 32:4,* TLB

Trust in the LORD with all your heart and lean not on your own understanding; in all your ways acknowledge him, and he will make your paths straight. *Proverbs 3:5-6,* NIV

Know therefore that the LORD your God, He is God, the faithful God, who keeps His covenant and His lovingkindness to a thousandth generation with those who love Him and keep His commandments . . . *Deuteronomy 7:9,* NASB

Because of the LORD's great love we are not consumed, for his compassions never fail. They are new every morning; great is your faithfulness. *Lamentations 3:22-23,* NIV

But the Lord is still in his holy temple; he still rules from heaven. He closely watches everything that happens here on earth. *Psalm 11:4,* TLB

Let us hold unswervingly to the hope we profess, for he who promised is faithful. *Hebrews 10:23,* NIV

Maintaining Your Body

"Glorify God in your body . . ."
ST. PAUL

I praise you because I am fearfully and wonderfully made; your works are wonderful, I know that full well. My frame was not hidden from you when I was made in the secret place. *Psalm 139:14-15a,* NIV

The LORD will guide you always; he will satisfy your needs in a sun-scorched land and will strengthen your frame. You will be like a well-watered garden, like a spring whose waters never fail. *Isaiah 58:11,* NIV

But I will restore you to health and heal your wounds, declares the LORD . . . *Jeremiah 30:17a,* NIV

Surely our griefs He Himself bore,
And our sorrows He carried;
Yet we ourselves esteemed
Him stricken,
Smitten of God, and afflicted.
But He was pierced through
for our transgressions,
He was crushed for our iniquities;
The chastening for our well-being

fell upon Him,
And by His scourging we are healed.
Isaiah 53:4-5, NASB

But for you who revere my name, the sun of righteousness will rise with healing in its wings. And you will go out and leap like calves released from the stall. *Malachi 4:2,* NIV

As a father has compassion on his children, so the LORD has compassion on those who fear him; for he knows how we are formed, he remembers that we are dust. *Psalm 103:13-14,* NIV

Cast your cares on the LORD and he will sustain you; he will never let the righteous fall. *Psalm 55:22,* NIV

Or do you not know that your body is a temple of the Holy Spirit who is in you, whom you have from God, and that you are not your own? For you have been bought with a price: therefore glorify God in your body. *1 Corinthians 6:19-20,* NASB

And my God shall supply all your needs according to His riches in glory in Christ Jesus. *Philippians 4:19,* NASB

Trust in the Lord God always, for in the Lord Jehovah is your everlasting strength. *Isaiah 26:4,* TLB

He gives strength to the weary,
And to him who lacks might
He increases power.
Though youths grow weary and tired,
And vigorous young men
stumble badly,
Yet those who wait for the LORD
Will gain new strength;
They will mount up with
wings like eagles,
They will run and not get tired,
They will walk and not become weary.
Isaiah 40:29-31, NASB

And so, dear brothers, I plead with you to give your bodies to God. Let them be a living sacrifice, holy—the kind he can accept. When you think of what he has done for you, is this too much to ask? *Romans 12:1, TLB*

But our citizenship is in heaven. And we eagerly await a Savior from there, the Lord Jesus Christ, who, by the power that enables him to bring everything under his control, will transform our lowly bodies so that they will be like his glorious body. *Philippians 3:20-21, NIV*

Facing the Future

"I said to the man who stood at the gate of the year: Give me a light that I may tread safely into the unknown. And he replied: Go out into the darkness, and put thine hand into the hand of God. That shall be to thee better than light and safer than a known way."

M. LOUISE HASKINS

"For I know the plans that I have for you," declares the LORD, "plans for welfare and not for calamity to give you a future and a hope." *Jeremiah 29:11*, NASB

You discern my going out and my lying down; you are familiar with all my ways . . . You hem me in—behind and before; you have laid your hand upon me. *Psalm 139:3, 5*, NIV

Don't be afraid, for the Lord will go before you and will be with you; he will not fail nor forsake you. *Deuteronomy 31:8*, TLB

"Have I not commanded you? Be strong and courageous! Do not tremble or be dismayed, for the LORD your God is with you wherever you go." *Joshua 1:9*, NASB

For this God is our God for ever and ever; he will be our guide even to the end. *Psalm 48:14*, NIV

The LORD is your keeper;
The LORD is your shade
on your right hand.
The sun will not smite you by day,
Nor the moon by night.
The LORD will protect you
from all evil;
He will keep your soul.
The LORD will guard your going out
and your coming in
From this time forth and forever.
Psalm 121:5-8, NASB

I will instruct you (says the Lord) and guide you along the best pathway for your life; I will advise you and watch your progress. *Psalm 32:8, TLB*

But when he, the Spirit of truth, comes, he will guide you into all truth. He will not speak on his own; he will speak only what he hears, and he will tell you what is yet to come. *John 16:13, NIV*

The steps of good men are directed by the Lord. He delights in each step they take. *Psalm 37:23, TLB*

Whether you turn to the right or to the left, your ears will hear a voice behind you, saying, "This is the way; walk in it." *Isaiah 30:21, NIV*

Trust in the LORD with all your heart and lean not on your own understanding; in all your ways acknowledge him, and he will make your paths straight. *Proverbs 3:5-6, NIV*

Other Pocketpac Books

BIBLE INDEX POCKETBOOK. This easy-to-read index contains references to more than 1000 important subjects. Useful with any translation.

THE BIBLE TELLS ME SO: God's Promises for Kids. The Bible's answers to questions kids ask most.

PARENT'S PROMISE POCKETBOOK. Hundreds of verses highlight the blessings and challenges of parenting.

PERSONAL PROMISE POCKETBOOK. Discover how God's promises and purposes correspond to many of your needs. The Four-Step System will help you claim and retain these verses.

POCKET GUIDE TO THE NEW TESTAMENT. Handy outlines and summaries of content and theological themes for each book of the New Testament.

POCKET GUIDE TO THE OLD TESTAMENT. Handy outlines and summaries of content and theological themes for each book of the Old Testament.

PROMISES FOR GRANDPARENTS. Strong comfort from Scripture for those who are growing older and want to build a godly heritage.

STUDENT' PROMISE POCKETBOOK. Special answers from God's Word for students and young adults, featuring the Four-Step System that helps you personalize and claims God's promises.